✦ CRITTI
✦ SHARK-✳
✳ CAM+

written by
MARGIE PALATINI

illustrated by
DAN YACCARINO

Ready-to-Read

SIMON SPOTLIGHT

New York   London   Toronto   Sydney   New Delhi

For Ruby
—M. P.

For Pinkie
—D. Y.

SIMON SPOTLIGHT
An imprint of Simon & Schuster Children's Publishing Division
1230 Avenue of the Americas, New York, New York 10020
This Simon Spotlight edition June 2023
Text copyright © 2023 by Margie Palatini
Illustrations copyright © 2023 by Dan Yaccarino
SIMON SPOTLIGHT, READY-TO-READ, and colophon are registered trademarks of Simon & Schuster, Inc.
For information about special discounts for bulk purchases, please contact Simon & Schuster Specials Sales
at 1-866-506-1949 or business@simonandschuster.com.
Manufactured in the United States of America 0523 LAK
2 4 6 8 10 9 7 5 3 1
This title was cataloged with the Library of Congress.
ISBN 978-1-6659-2735-2 (hc)
ISBN 978-1-6659-2734-5 (pbk)
ISBN 978-1-6659-2736-9 (ebook)

Swim, Shark. Swim.

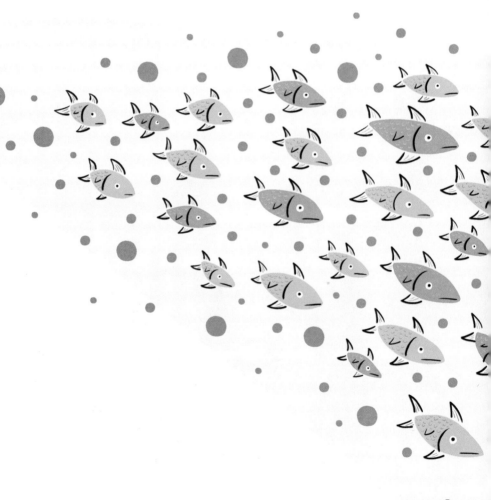

Swim.

Swim.

Swim.

Sad. Very sad.

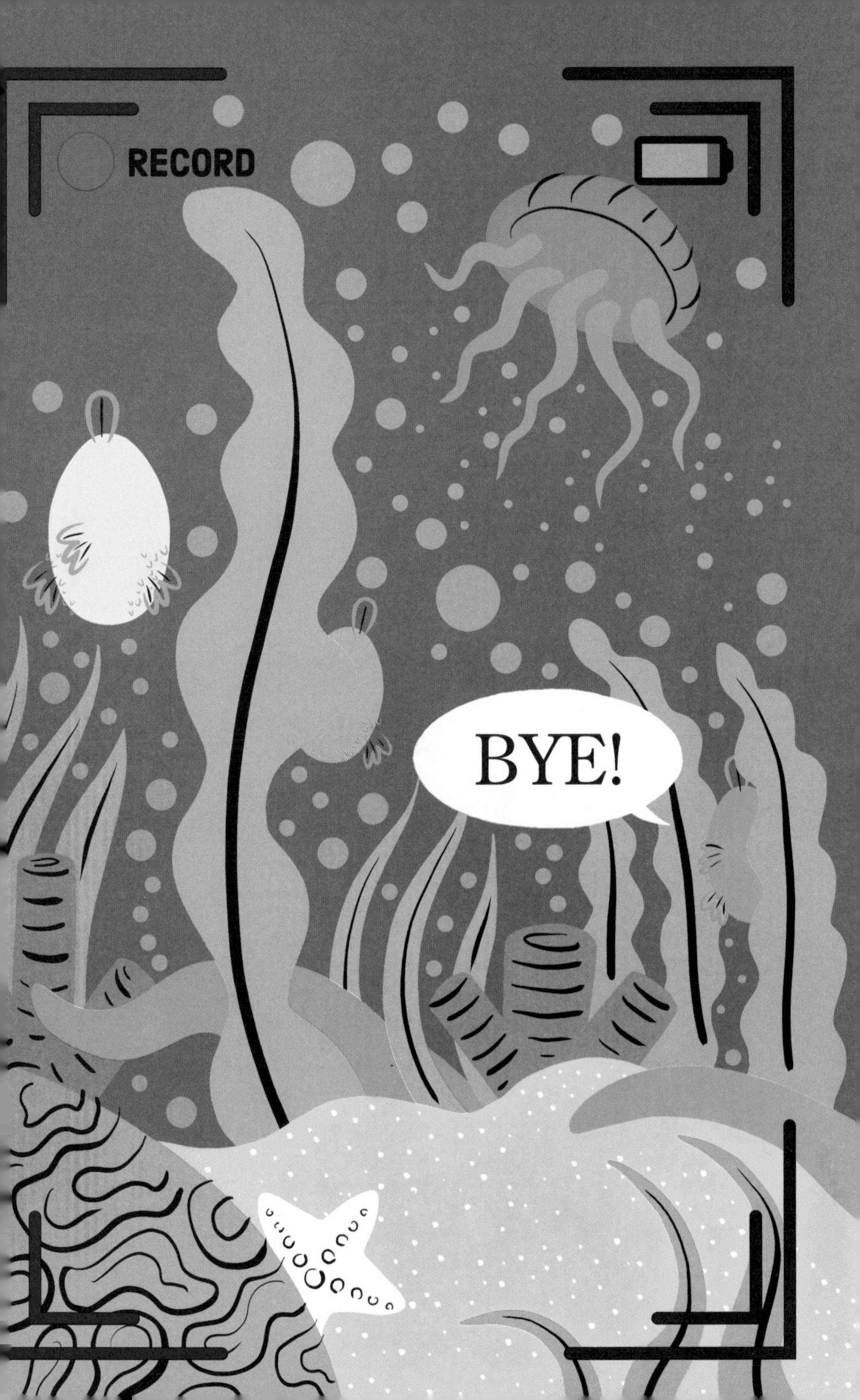
RECORD
BYE!

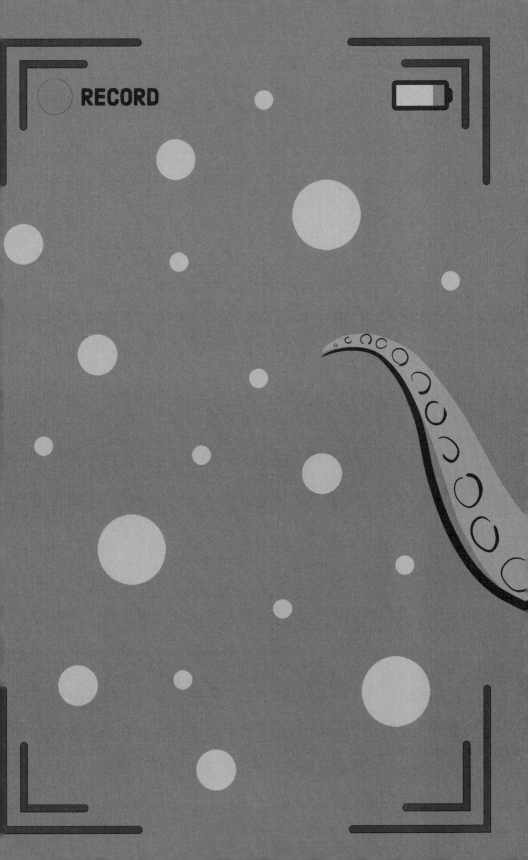

Swing. Sway.

RECORD

Whoa!

 RECORD

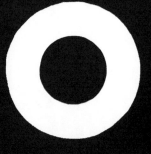

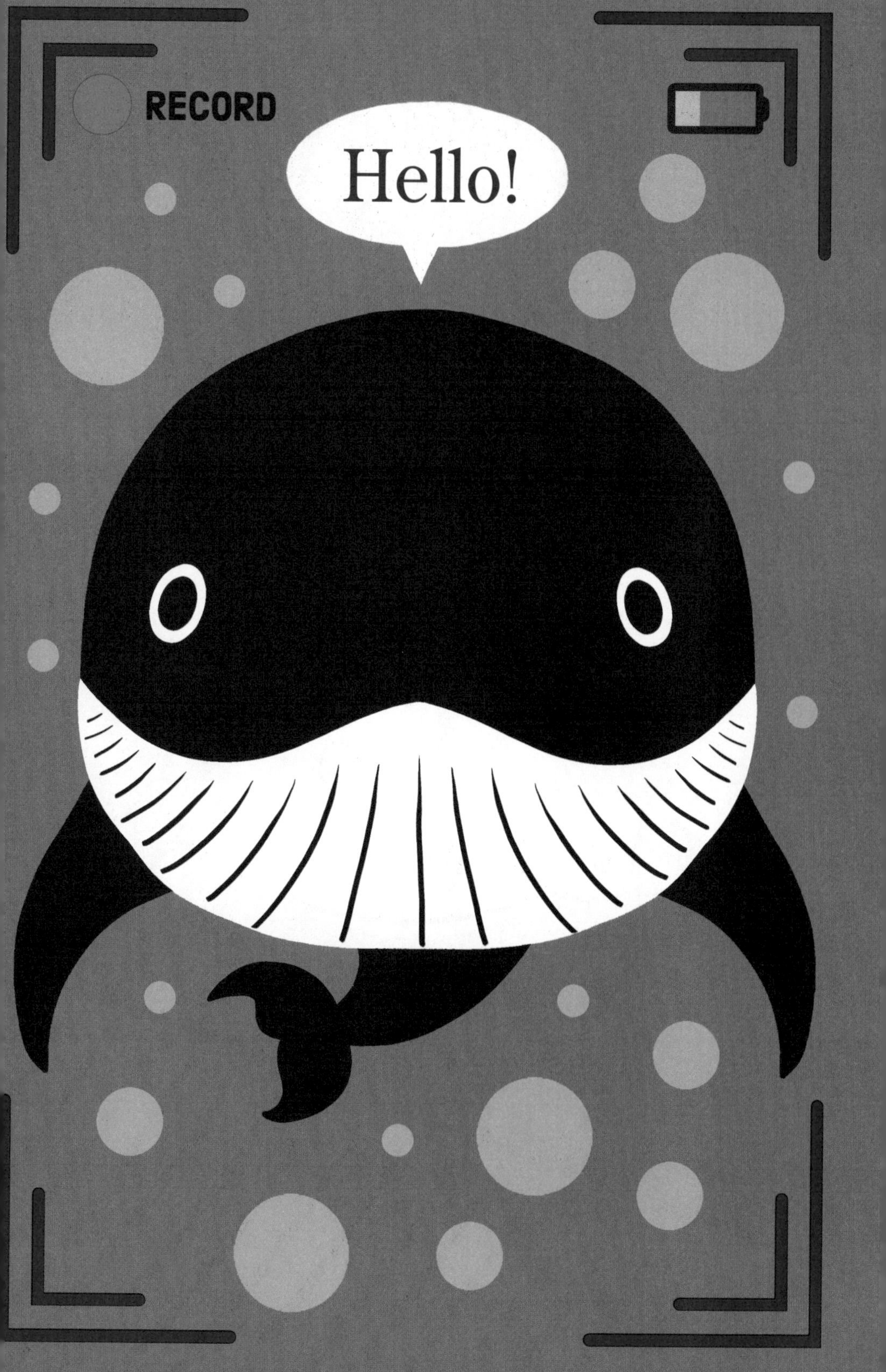
RECORD
Hello!

WHOOSH!

Dark.

Dark.

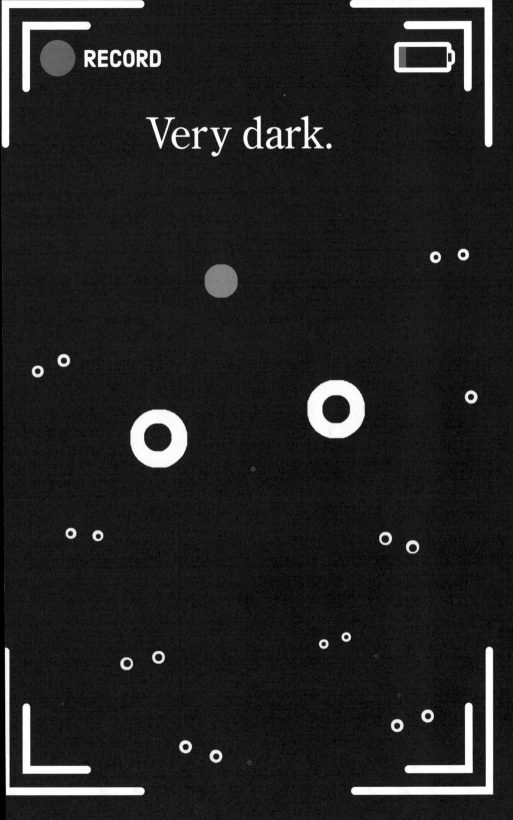

RECORD

Very dark.

Everybody, swim!
Swim. Swim. Swim.

Whew!
Tired. Tired. Tired.

And hungry!

RECORD

Party on, Shark!